17 Kings and 42 Elephants

First published in the United States 1987 by
Dial Books for Young Readers
A Division of Penguin Books USA Inc.
375 Hudson Street New York, New York 10014

Published in Great Britain by J.M. Dent & Sons Ltd.
Original edition first published in 1972
This edition (reillustrated) first published in 1987
Text copyright © 1972 by Margaret Mahy
Pictures copyright © 1987 by Patricia MacCarthy
All rights reserved
Library of Congress Catalog Card Number: 87-5311
Printed in Hong Kong by South China Printing Company (1988) Limited
First Pied Piper Printing 1990
N
1 3 5 7 9 10 8 6 4 2

A Pied Piper Book is a registered trademark of
Dial Books for Young Readers,
a division of Penguin Books USA Inc.,
® TM 1,163,686 and ® TM 1,054,312.

17 KINGS AND 42 ELEPHANTS
is published in a hardcover edition by
Dial Books for Young Readers.
ISBN 0-8037-0781-9

The art for this book consists of batik paintings on silk,
which were then color-separated and reproduced in full color.

17 Kings and 42 Elephants

Margaret Mahy

pictures by Patricia MacCarthy

Dial Books for Young Readers · New York

Seventeen kings on forty-two elephants
Going on a journey through a wild wet night,

Baggy ears like big umbrellaphants,
Little eyes a-gleaming in the jungle light.

Seventeen kings saw white-toothed crocodiles
Romping in the river where the reeds grow tall,

Green-eyed dragons, rough as rockodiles,
Lying in the mud where the small crabs crawl.

Forty-two elephants – oh, what a lot of 'ums,
Big feet beating in the wet wood shade,

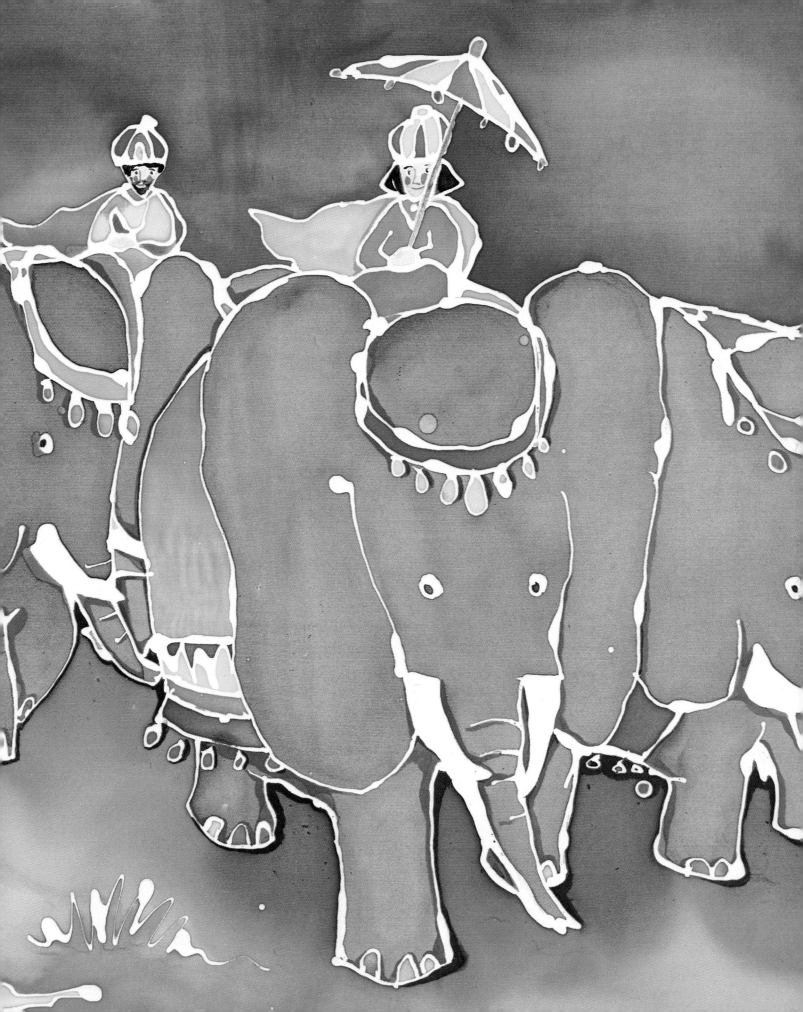

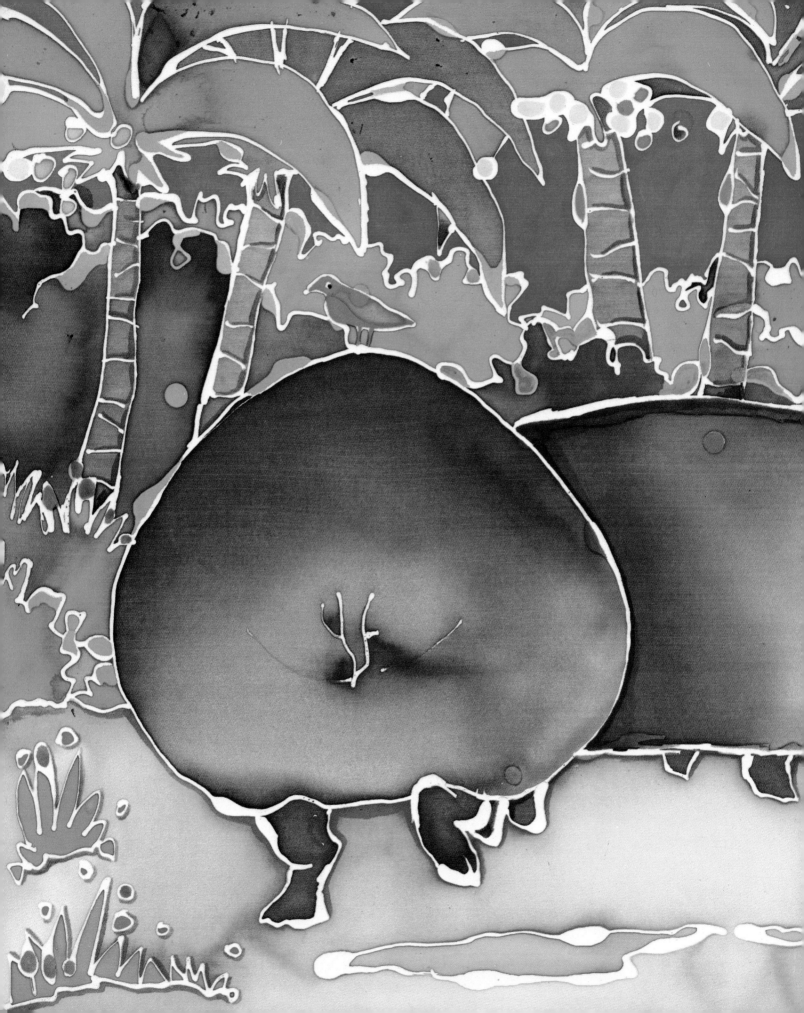

Proud and ponderous hippopotomums
Danced to the music that the marchers made.

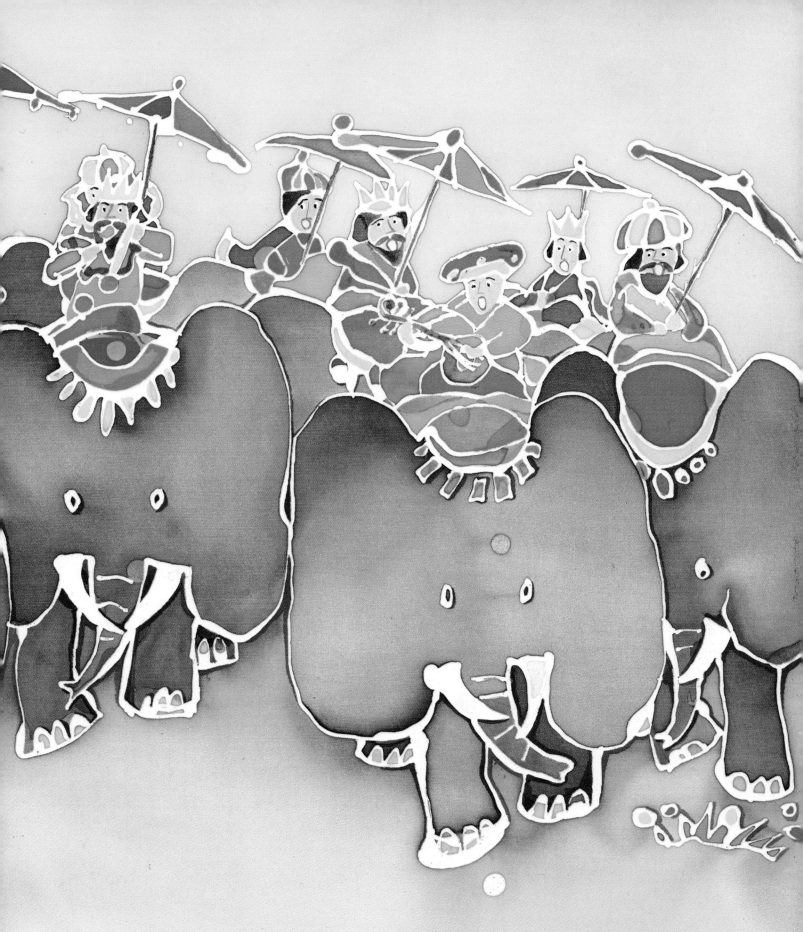

Seventeen kings sang loud and happily,
Forty-two elephants swayed to the song.

Tigers at the riverside drinking lappily,
Knew the kings were happy as they marched along.

Who joined the singsong? Cranes and pelicans,
Peacocks fluttering their fine fantails,

Flamingos chanting "Ding Dong Bellicans!"
Rosy as a garden in the jungle vales.

Tinkling tunesters, twangling trillicans,
Butterflied and fluttered by the great green trees.

Big baboonsters, black gorillicans
Swinging from the branches by their hairy knees.

Kings in crimson, crowns all crystalline,
Moving to the music of a single gong.

Watchers in the jungle, moist and mistalline,
Bibble-bubble-babbled to the bing-bang-bong!

Seventeen kings – the heavy night swallowed them,
Raindrops glistened on the elephants' backs.

Nobody stopped them, nobody followed them –
The deep dark jungle has devoured their tracks.